Happy Again

by Al Webster
illustrated by Debbie Mourtzios

Harcourt
SCHOOL PUBLISHERS

Printed in China

ISBN 10: 0-15-351429-9
ISBN 13: 978-0-15-351429-6

Ordering Options
ISBN 10: 0-15-351212-1 (Grade 2 Advanced Collection)
ISBN 13: 978-0-15-351212-4 (Grade 2 Advanced Collection)
ISBN 10: 0-15-358064-X (package of 5)
ISBN 13: 978-0-15-358064-2 (package of 5)

5 6 7 8 9 10   985   15 14 13 12 11 10 09

For a week, it rained constantly.

"I'm tired of being stuck inside," sighed Lisa. "It's so boring."

"It's *really* boring," said Toby.

"At least our house is warm and dry," said Mom. "Not everyone is as lucky."

Down the hill at the end of their street, the river rose so high that it flooded Mr. Cowan's house. Mr. Cowan had to leave his home and move into a hotel until the water went back down.

When Mr. Cowan returned to his house a few days later, most of his furniture had been spoiled by the water. He was very upset, so his neighbors took him warm blankets, food supplies, and other items.

Toby and his dad bought Mr. Cowan a comfortable chair to replace his ruined one. "What a good bargain!" said Dad.

Toby and Dad delivered the chair to
Mr. Cowan's house.

"How thoughtful of you!" said Mr.
Cowan, but he still looked extremely upset.

"I think he is worried that his house
might flood again," said Dad.

6

Mom said, "Let's have a party for
Mr. Cowan on Saturday to cheer him up."
"I can sing," said Lisa.
"I want to sing, too," said Toby.

On the day of the party, Dad baked
his famous strawberry cake. Lisa and Toby
rehearsed their song in the living room
while Mom made cardboard ears, paws,
and a velvet tail for Toby. She stuffed the
tail to make it firm.

8

On Saturday afternoon, lots of neighbors arrived at Mr. Cowan's house for the party. Mr. Cowan showed them into the living room. They put the food that they had brought on the coffee table and exchanged stories about the flood.

Lisa and Toby came forward, and Lisa gave Toby a boost up onto a wide window ledge. She was about to sing when Mr. Cowan had to answer the door. They waited a few minutes until he came back into the room, smiling and holding a letter in his hand.

Then Lisa sang an old song about a dog in a shop window. Some of the neighbors sang along with the chorus, and Toby said, "Woof, woof!" at the end of each line.

Each time Toby said, "Woof, woof!" he held up his paws. Suddenly, Lisa saw Mr. Cowan wasn't just smiling. He was laughing out loud along with everyone else.

After the singing finished, Mr. Cowan showed everyone the letter that had been delivered. He said, "The mayor has offered me a new house away from the river. I will never have to worry about the floods again."

All the neighbors cheered.

"Thank you for organizing this marvelous party," Mr. Cowan said. "I would like you all to visit me in my new house."

He patted Toby on the head and said, "Please bring this dog. He reminded me how to laugh."

"Woof, woof!" barked Toby.

Everyone laughed, and then they enjoyed the food together.

14

Think Critically

1. What happened to Mr. Cowan during the story?

2. Describe Mr. Cowan's feelings after the flood compared to after the party.

3. What words could you use to describe Mr. Cowan's neighbors?

4. Read page 9. What word could you use instead of *exchanged*?

5. What is something you could do for someone who is feeling sad?

 **Social Studies**

Write a Letter Think about why the mayor may have offered Mr. Cowan a new house. Then write a letter like the one that Mr. Cowan may have received from the mayor. Include the mayor's reasons for offering Mr. Cowan a new house in the community.

School-Home Connection Think about someone you know who has been feeling sad. Write them a letter or draw them a picture to cheer them up.

Word Count: 486